What does it mean?

What does it mean?

I'M SORRY

by Susan Riley

THE CHILD'S WORLD

ELGIN, ILLINOIS 60120

Art prepared by Collateral, Inc.

Distributed by Childrens Press, 1224 West Van Buren Street, Chicago, Illinois 60607.

Library of Congress Cataloging in Publication Data

Riley, Sue, 1946-
  Sorry.

  (What does it mean?)
  SUMMARY: Identifies occasions when one may "feel sorry," such as being late, illness, and spilling milk.
  1. Sadness—Juvenile literature. [1. Conduct of life] I. Title.
BF575.G7R55   170′.202′22   77-16811
ISBN 0-89565-013-4

I didn't make it.
It's past time for our date.

I'm sorry to keep you waiting.
Sorry to be late.

Here I come now
as fast as I can.
I'm sorry, I'm sorry.
I'll say it again.

Have you ever been sorry
for something you've done?
Or have you ever
felt sorry for anyone?

I feel sorry for people
when they are sick.
I say, "Sorry you're sick.
Get well quick."

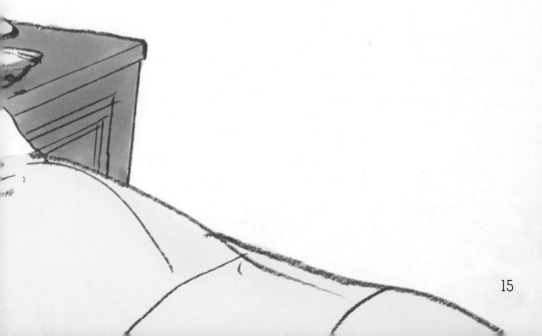

I feel sorry for my friend
whenever he cries.

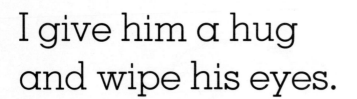

I give him a hug
and wipe his eyes.

And sometimes I'm sorry
for things that I do.
I say, "I'm sorry I did that.
I didn't mean to."

If I
spill my
milk
or
break a glass,

or jump in a puddle
and make a big splash,

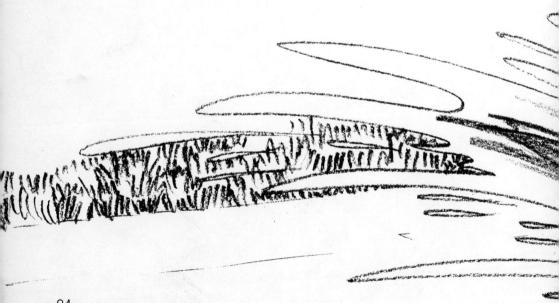

I always say,
"I'm sorry." I really do.
"I'm sorry" means, "I'll
try to do better," too.

Remember to say
you're sorry—
just like me.

Saying "sorry" makes
everyone feel better,
you see.

Books in this series